silly Millies

What Do You Do on a Farm?

Susan E. Goodman

Illustrated by Steve Pica

The Millbrook Press
Brookfield, Connecticut

To Jean—great to work for,
even better to work with

Copyright © 2002 by Susan E. Goodman
Illustrations copyright © 2002 by Steve Pica

Reading Consultant: Lea M. McGee

Silly Millies and the Silly Millies logo are trademarks
of The Millbrook Press, Inc.

Library of Congress Cataloging-in-Publication Data
Goodman, Susan.
What do you do on a farm? / Susan E. Goodman ;
illustrated by Steve Pica.
p. cm. — (Silly Millies)
Summary: Having been asked by a farmer to help feed and care for various
farm animals, a girl discovers a variety of facts about their diet and
behavior as she meets each one.
ISBN 0-7613-2756-8 (lib. binding) ISBN 0-7613-1786-4 (pbk.)
 [1. Domestic animals—Fiction.] I. Pica, Steve, ill. II. Title. III. Series.
PZ7.G61444 Wh 2002   [E]—dc21   2001006482

Published by The Millbrook Press, Inc.
2 Old New Milford Road
Brookfield, Connecticut 06804
www.millbrookpress.com

"Help me," says
the farmer.

3

"We need some eggs," he says.

What do you do?

You do not go to the store.

You go to the hen house.

7

You find eggs in the hay.
You go near the last hen.
You hear a "PEEP!"

What do you do?

You see a new chick.

You can't eat *that* egg for breakfast!

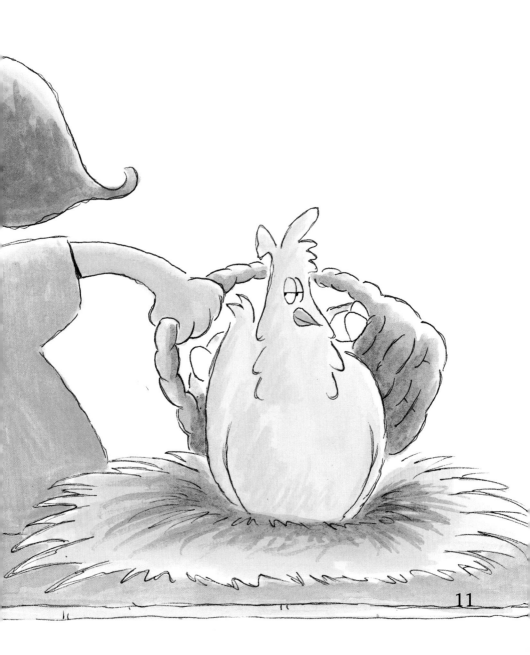

The farmer gives you a hose.
"The pigs are hot," he says.

What do you do?

Do not wet the pigs.

Put the water on the dirt.

Pigs roll in mud to stay cool.

The cow needs some food.

What do you do?

You give her some hay.
Then you grab the hose.
Cows drink a lot of water.

25

GALLONS

19

The new calf wants some food, too.

What do you do?

Nothing.

His mom gives him milk.

Now YOU want some food.

Listen. The dinner bell is ringing.

What do you do?

Eggs from the hens.

Milk from the cows.

Apples and melons.

Corn and cakes.

What do you do?

Dig in, of course!

You eat and eat.

Then you have only one bite left…

What do you do?

Dear Parents:

Congratulations! By sharing this book with your child, you are taking an important step in helping him or her become a good reader. *What Can You Do on a Farm?* is perfect for the child who can read with help. Below are some ideas for making sure your child's reading experience is a positive one.

TIPS FOR READING
- If your child knows most of the alphabet, begin by reading the book aloud, pausing every page or so to talk about the pictures. Point to the words as you read. When your child is familiar with the book, pause before the end of a sentence to see if your child will supply the word. Play word and letter games. For example, have your child point to words that begin with the same letter of the alphabet. Or write a word from the book on a card and see if your child can find it in the book.
- If your child knows how to read some words and knows the "sounds" of some letters, invite your child to read aloud to you. If your child does not know a word or reads it incorrectly, help by asking "What word do you think it will be?" or "Does that word make sense?" Encourage your child to look to the pictures for word clues. Or point to the first letter (or first two letters) of the word. If your child is stumped, pronounce the word slowly, running your finger underneath the letters.
- Encourage your child to reread the book. This builds confidence and gradually your child will be able to read without your help. Remember to provide lots of praise for the hard work of your early reader.

TIPS FOR DISCUSSION
- Ask your child what kinds of animals are found on a farm? How are they different from zoo animals? What does each animal contribute to the farm?
- Have your child imagine what it would be like to live and work on a farm. How would it differ from his or her life now?

Lea M. McGee, Ed.D.
Professor, Literacy Education
University of Alabama